T0144044

FARMER BARNABY FRED

By Madelyn Anderson

Written by Madelyn Anderson

Illustrated by Gary Bartholomew

Published by Madelyn Anderson

Balboa Press books may be ordered through booksellers or by contacting:

Balboa Press
A Division of Hay House
1663 Liberty Drive
Bloomington, IN 47403
www.balboapress.com
1 (877) 407-4847

ISBN: 978-1-9822-1189-9 (sc)
ISBN: 978-1-9822-1188-2 (e)

Print information available on the last page.

Balboa Press rev. date: 09/11/2018

Dedication

Caryn, Mike, Chloe, Elizabeth, Brodie, Beau and Rowan

While working one day,
Farmer Barnaby Fred
had a bundle *of* hay
fall on his head
and the doctor put Barnaby
right into bed

"You just rest, Barnaby"
said Dr. :Sneed.
"a good sleep right now
will be just what you need
the barnyard will run
along smoothly indeed.

HOME
IS WHERE
YOUR
HOUSE
IS

So Farmer Barnaby
Fred fell asleep and
immediately
started to count all his
sheep
but all of his sheep
were asleep in a heap

So Barnaby Fred
ran straight to the barn
and saw all the cows
knitting earmuffs
with yarn
and they asked if he had
any socks they
could darn

Barnaby Fred thought
Something was strange
The horses were singing
"Home on the Range"
This barnyard had
Certainly been through
A change

The piggies were taking
A bath in their pens
The rooster played
Tennis with some of the hens
And the donkey could
Count to 100 by 10's

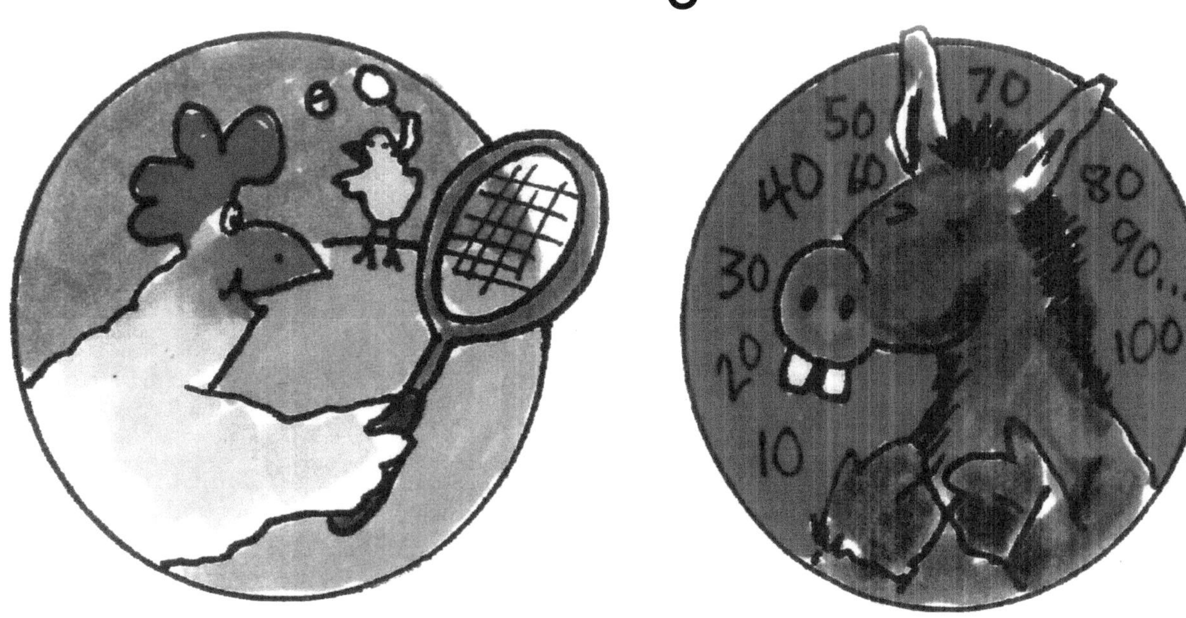

The ducks and the
turkeys were cooking up
lunch
and the St. Bernard dog
made a tasty fruit punch
What a certainly
different, unusual bunch!

Then all of a sudden
Barnaby Fred,
started blinking his eyes
and woke and said,
"I must have been
dreaming from bumping
my head"

He looked
out the window and saw
with a smile
that the barnyard was
running in fine barnyard
style
and he hoped it would
stay that way
for quite a while

Thanks For Reading

What crazy things do you dream about?

Maybe you have a story to share

Madelyn Anderson loves to cook and invent her own recipes, garden and fill her days with giggles alongside her grand kids, nieces and nephews

Printed in the United States
By Bookmasters